D0576156

BOATBUILDER

written and photographed by Hope Herman Wurmfeld

MACMILLAN PUBLISHING COMPANY   NEW YORK
COLLIER MACMILLAN PUBLISHERS   LONDON

Many thanks for the kindness and patience of the able boatbuilders at the boatyard of Ralph W. Stanley, Inc., Southwest Harbor, Maine, and to the Stanley family; to Alex and his father; to the Hinckley Co. of Southwest Harbor, who generously introduced me to Ralph; and to Jeremy, who accompanied me on some of my journeys and was always with me in spirit.

Copyright © 1988 by Hope Wurmfeld
All rights reserved. No part of this book may be reproduced or transmitted
in any form or by any means, electronic or mechanical, including photocopying, recording,
or by any information storage and retrieval system, without permission in writing from the Publisher.
Macmillan Publishing Company
866 Third Avenue, New York, NY 10022
Collier Macmillan Canada, Inc.
First Edition
Printed in the United States of America

10 9 8 7 6 5 4 3 2 1

The text of this book is set in 14 point Simoncini Garamond.
The illustrations are black-and-white photographs reproduced in halftone.

Library of Congress Cataloging-in-Publication Data
Wurmfeld, Hope Herman.
Boatbuilder/by Hope Herman Wurmfeld. – 1st ed.   p.   cm.
ISBN 0-02-793580-9
1. Friendship sloops – Design and construction. 2. Stanley, Ralph W.
3. Boatbuilding – Maine. I. Title.
VM311.F7W87 1988   623.8'223'0924 – dc19
87-21153   CIP   AC

To my father,
Charles H. Herman

There is a land in the northeast corner of the United States that is as rewarding as it is difficult. It is a land of contrasts—pine forests, high mountains, rocky headlands. Here on the coast mountaintops receive the first rays of sun on the North American continent. And here the tidal variation may be as great as forty feet. A myriad of small islands like a galaxy of stars edge the land and provide a network of salt marshes and bogs for Canadian geese, wading birds, water fowl, and puffins. Lobster, cod, and sea scallops abound, and salmon spawn in the fresh, fast-moving waters of the Kennebec and Penobscot rivers. Flowers bloom with an uncommon brilliance.

Bath, Boothbay, Friendship, Southwest Harbor—here, for as long as anyone can remember, coastal families have been part of the life of the sea. In the rains of April and in the fierce storms of September, in fog and in freezing snow, whatever the season or whatever the weather, the fishing boats have gone out. In spite of the difficulties of life in a land so challenging, the people have survived and even thrived. They are strong and resourceful.

Down East, along the coast of Maine from islands near the Canadian border to sheltered harbors farther south, there is a boatbuilder whom everybody knows. His name is Ralph Stanley, and he is a man of the sea, as were his father and grandfather and great-grandfather before him. Ralph Stanley is a sailor and a master builder of wooden boats.

From the time he was a very young man, Ralph knew he wanted to be a builder of wooden boats. He was always designing boats and making models and thinking about how boats sailed and how they looked in the water. Ralph thought about boatbuilding all the time.

"In those days," he says, "the only way to learn was by watching. Each builder had his secrets of the trade that were carefully guarded. You couldn't ask questions, because they would never tell it quite right."

So Ralph Stanley watched. He quietly made small sketches and took notes for himself. After several years of apprenticeship, he felt ready to set out on his own. His family did not discourage him, but they were not convinced that boatbuilding in a small village would be profitable. They loved Ralph and did not want to see him struggle.

Many years have passed. Now Ralph Stanley has a successful boatyard humming with the sound of bandsaws and sanding machines and smelling of fresh paint. People come from far and wide to exchange ideas and to commission the building of new boats.

Today Ralph has a large family of his own. He and his wife, Marion, have many children and grandchildren who live close by. At various times they all come to help out in the "yard." The boatyard of Ralph W. Stanley, Inc., is a family venture sparked by this man's dreams and skill.

The Stanley boatyard sits on the edge of the Atlantic Ocean in Southwest Harbor, a sheltered inlet of Mt. Desert Island on the coast of Maine. The Stanley yard repairs and restores boats and also builds new ones. Building new boats is only one of many kinds of projects undertaken in an active boatyard like this one. There are sheds for storing boats in winter, a machine shop for making repairs with enough space for the construction of new boats, and ways, or skids, for launching vessels into the sea.

Venture, Endeavor, Peregrine, Freedom, Morning Star—these are the names of some of the vessels in winter storage at the Stanley yard. After a summer of sailing, wooden boats must dry out in a well-aired shed. Salt and barnacles are removed while the bottom of the boat is still wet. People trust Ralph's shop to take care of their boats and repair them, if necessary, in time for the next season.

Sometimes the repairs on an old wooden boat are very extensive. New parts must be made to replace those that are missing or defective. So much work may be involved that it is not a repair at all, but a rebuilding or a restoration.

It is seven in the morning. A thin curl of white smoke and the scent of burning pine come from a small woodstove in a corner of the machine shop. On a low bench rests a brown bag of freshly baked doughnuts. Richard, Ralph's son, and Tim, his son-in-law, stand beside the stove warming their hands. Tanya, a young apprentice, comes in a few minutes later with Lang, a golden retriever who sometimes visits.

Ralph's staff has been trained at a school for boatbuilding. Here at Ralph's yard they have a chance to use and develop their skills. Sanding, painting, checking boats for leaks, receiving a delivery of wood—these are some of the tasks for the day.

If there are unusual weather conditions, other work in the yard must wait. When a hurricane is forecast, masts must be taken off and sails and booms removed. Smaller boats are taken out of the water at high tide and hauled into one of the several large sheds. The larger boats remain afloat but must be secured with extra line.

One day Ralph receives a phone call from an old friend. He would like the yard to build a new boat for his son. Because a boat must reflect the needs and spirit of its owner, Ralph listens carefully and asks many questions. He knows who will be sailing the boat, but in what kind of water? Does the sailor plan to sail solo or with friends most of the time? Will he handle the vessel alone or depend on a crew? Will he sail in the sea or on inland waterways? All of these factors must be considered carefully.

Ralph has known the family a long time. They spend summers on an island close to Southwest Harbor and often come to town. He knows that his friend's son, Alex, has been sailing from the time he was small and is a fine sailor. Father and son would like a boat built from the white oak trees of Maine, a boat in the tradition of the Down East working boats of the coast, not fancy but

strong and fast, a boat to sail in the coves and bays around the small island where they summer.

Since Alex is leaving shortly for school, it is decided that he and Ralph will correspond. Ralph will send sketches and plans to both Alex and his father. Some weeks later, Ralph receives a letter.

Dear Ralph,

I hope you and the family are well and that the yard is busy. School is school. What can I say? I think a lot about Maine and my new boat. I forget whether my dad mentioned that I really like the idea of taking off by myself, sailing for a couple of days with only the wind and the sea and the boat for company, with just a sleeping bag and some cooking stuff in the hold.

My best regards to everyone.

Alex

Ralph has been thinking about the new boat and answers Alex's letter immediately. He has the perfect solution: a day sailer along the lines of the old fishing vessels that were originally built in Friendship, Maine. Alex's boat would be nineteen feet long and could easily be managed single-handed.

Alex and his father are enthusiastic about Ralph's proposal. Alex's father writes to Ralph, "I know those old fishing boats were designed for safety, speed, and ease of handling, exactly what is needed here. Let's plan to go ahead as soon as possible."

It is time for the annual sloop races hosted by the Bath (Maine) Maritime Museum. Ralph decides to postpone boatbuilding for a week, to race one of the wooden boats that he has rebuilt, the *Morning Star*. He and Marion sail down the coast to see old friends and compete in the regatta at Boothbay and Friendship.

Ever since Ralph first heard stories about his great, great-grandfather who shipped out to see the world in a schooner from Gloucester, Massachusetts, Ralph has been fascinated by these vessels and the fishing boats that developed from them, called Friendship sloops.

Not everyone agrees how the first Friendships developed. Some people think that the prototypes of the early sloops were larger vessels that sailed out of Gloucester. Ralph thinks that although there was certainly influence from Gloucester, the boats themselves were designed for Maine coastal conditions.

Whatever changes have taken place over the years, there is a basic outline to a Friendship sloop that makes it easy to recognize. It has the look of a working boat. Like a well-conditioned athlete, it is sturdy, strong, and graceful. It is the traditional fishing vessel of the Maine coast.

Early in the morning on the day of the race at Boothbay, Ralph and Marion row to shore from the *Morning Star*. Although the races are competitive, they are held in a spirit of camaraderie and fun. There is a trophy for the sloop with the youngest member aboard, one for the middle of the fleet, and one for the sloop that has traveled the farthest in order to take part in the regatta. For the skippers, it is a time to use their boats and push them a little and think about the early days of sail, when it was important to be fast at sea.

At the skippers' meeting before the race, there is a review of the course. The boats will race around the designated buoys and will start and finish at the same point. It is to be a closed-course race. A closed-course race is usually short enough to be sailed in a morning or an afternoon of racing.

An important item on the agenda is the coastal waters forecast provided by the National Weather Service out of Portland. "Today will be beautiful," the commodore informs the group. "The sky is blue. The sun is shining. What you see is what you'll get. It's not going to rain today, I promise you. Winds are running out of the southwest at about seventeen knots. There is a fresh breeze and probably a light chop with some long southwest swells. It's a great day for sailing. Now, good luck to all of you. Have a good race and a good sail."

"How about tomorrow's sail to Friendship?" asks one of the skippers.

"There's a hurricane off the Carolinas," replies the commodore. "It has been downgraded to a tropical storm, but is expected to go offshore and re-form. It is going to influence our weather tomorrow. Keep advised. Tomorrow morning we are going to take a long, hard look at the weather and decide just what we are going to do about our trip over to Friendship."

"Ready about! Hard alee," Ralph calls as everyone on the *Morning Star* ducks and braces.

"Keep your head clear of the boom," Ralph shouts as he rounds the first bell buoy at Spruce Point. Marion tightens the sheets to starboard. Ralph's strategy for the first marker is to stay as close to the shoreline as they can for as long as possible, for better winds and less tide.

The next marker at Cuckold Ledge is the farthest point in the nine-mile race. *Morning Star* is in front, ahead of *Eagle, Sazarac,* and *Voyager*, three other sloops in her class. Once away, Ralph and Marion check their chart. Where next? Around a buoy at Fisherman's Island Passage that marks a ledge fourteen inches beneath the water. Be careful! They're running before the wind, with *Voyager* and *Eagle* closely following.

At the next-to-last marker *Voyager* and *Morning Star* are poised to start around the buoy. Who will go first? There is a moment of hesitation that seems like an eternity. In reality it is only part of a minute. Who has the wind? *Morning Star* is to windward! *Voyager* must give her buoy room.

In the final run toward the finish line, it's *Morning Star* in front, with *Eagle* and *Sazarac* close behind. Boom! The cannon signal on the committee boat goes off in a puff of black smoke. Ralph and Marion are first over the finish line. The *Morning Star* has won her race!

"What is it that makes one Friendship sloop faster than another?" someone asks Ralph.

"The shape," he answers.

"How are they different?"

"They are all the same shape," Ralph replies with a twinkle in his eye. "But there are subtle differences. It all depends on how you sail her."

"But, Ralph, why does the *Morning Star* win so often in her class?"

"It's hard to say exactly," Ralph says. "I built her a little differently from the way she originally was. I designed her with as much sail as it was possible to put on."

Awards for the day's races are given in each of several categories. Friendship sloops from different eras compete with each other rather than with the entire fleet. The *Morning Star* is in class A, a category of wooden Friendships built before 1921. The other categories are for boats constructed after 1921 and include those built of fiberglass.

"And now, announces the commodore, the award for first place in class A. These are the originals and are what our sloop society is all about. The first place in class A goes to a man who has put more masts in this harbor than anybody else. A builder and a skipper—the captain of the *Morning Star,* Ralph Stanley!"

"Hear, hear!" Everyone applauds as Ralph makes his way to the front to receive his trophy. Ralph has won in his category for the past five years. He accepts the award with a smile and a handshake and sits down quickly next to Marion.

After all the trophies are awarded, Ralph plays his fiddle, and the captains and their families eat a fish chowder supper and talk until late at night.

Sometimes Ralph will be asked why he builds in wood when fiberglass is just as durable and easier to maintain.

"More fun, I guess," Ralph says. "Wood gets better as it ages." And then he adds, "Besides, it's the old way. People have been building boats of wood for a long, long time, and I like to think that I am part of that tradition. Every wooden boat is different—like people—and I always learn something new."

By this time a rather large group has gathered around Ralph, but he is so engrossed in his thoughts that he hardly notices. Only when he stops briefly does he become aware of his audience and decide that it is time to get some chowder.

Next morning aboard the *Morning Star,* Ralph hears the blast of the foghorn off Crown's Point before his eyes are open. When he comes on deck, he sees a dark sky and almost impenetrable fog. No race today, he thinks, but you can never tell. The sun might burn off the fog by midmorning.

Again, he and Marion row to shore for the skippers' meeting.

The commodore is holding the coastal waters forecast and shaking his head. "No race today, but if it clears by tomorrow, we are going to try to get to Friendship. We'll see you tomorrow morning right here in the boathouse."

After the races at Boothbay and Friendship, it is time to get back to boat-building. During his week away, Ralph has had time to think about the new boat for Alex. He has a good understanding of the way Alex likes to sail and has considered the safety factors he will build into the design.

Now Ralph is ready to think about shape. He knows how he wants the boat to look as it sits in the water, the proportion of length to width and the curve of the sides of the hull.

The boat for Alex will be a nineteen-footer, the first in what Ralph hopes will be a series of sailboats of this size and shape. They will be known as Stanley 19's. For extra stability, as in the typical sloop boats, the Stanley 19 will be wide, approximately 8½ feet at her greatest beam, with ballast of lead inside. For a feeling of greater control, Alex wants a tiller instead of a wheel. There will be no centerboard. The boat will be a relatively deep-draught vessel, which means the keel will go down deep. The sail plan will be conservative in comparison to the size of the boat, for additional safety and ease of handling alone.

Ralph makes a plan, called a lines drawing, of the Stanley 19. This is a set of drawings that defines a boat—its shape, size, and relationships of parts. Once the lines drawing has been completed, it's time to begin to build.

The floor of the largest shed must be carefully swept. All sawdust and wood scrapings are removed. When everything is clean and smooth, plywood boards are set down. The lines of the vessel are drawn full-scale on the boards. The process of drawing the lines of the vessel to actual size is called "lofting" because in the past the lines were set down in the attic or loft of a barn or large shed.

"Fairing the lines" in boatbuilding means making curved lines accurately, without bulges or bumps. One device that Ralph uses to help make the curve precise is a flexible piece of wood called a batten. Nails are hammered into the lofting board on either side of the batten to hold it to the desired curve. After Ralph draws the curve, he removes the nails and the batten. In boatbuilding, a smooth curve is referred to as "fair."

From the full-scale drawing, Ralph will make molds that are to be set across the keel.

The molds are made from a number of boards cut to the proper curve and shape and screwed and nailed together.

When the molds are complete, they are placed on the keel in their proper location and so define the shape of the hull.

Hardwood from slow-growing trees, the white oak trees of Maine, makes sound, durable timber for the keel. Great care is taken with the keel, for it is the foundation upon which the rest of the boat is built.

The keel is made of several parts that are glued and bolted together. Ralph and his helpers are very careful and work a long time on the alignment and smoothness of each section of keel. They adjust and readjust the placement of horn timber and sternpost. The parts must be lined up straight and without space between them. After Ralph is satisfied with the fit, each piece is given two coats of wood preservative and a coat of bedding compound. This helps to prevent water and air from reaching the joints and thus retards potential rot.

Then the sections of keel are clamped together to complete the seal. Bronze bolts, made on a die at the shop, are put into place so that the clamps may be removed. The completed keel is set on blocks at the angle at which it is going to float in the water. It must be set up vertically and level at its waterline.

Notches along the upper edge of the keel are called rabbets. The rabbets are trimmed with an adze to allow for a smooth fit of the planking on the keel.

Ralph positions the hole for the rudder post in the horn timber.

Richard measures for accurate placement of the stopwaters, softwood dowels that are placed between the joints of keel members to keep water out.

Finally, when the keel is complete, it is ready for the molds.

Once the molds are in place, the keel and the molds must be rigidly braced by a series of supports and countersupports. There are supports on either side of the keel. The molds are held in place by uprights to the ceiling. The entire unit is braced from above and held tightly to the keel by a device called a Spanish windlass. The Spanish windlass holds a vertical and horizontal line taut and allows for further tightening when necessary.

After the molds are set on top of the keel, long strips of flexible, freshly cut green spruce are curved around the molds fore and aft. These strips of wood are called ribbands and mark the longitudinal shape of the boat. The ribbands provide a form against which the ribs will be placed.

Starting at the top and alternating sides, single-length pieces of wood are placed lengthwise from eight to ten inches apart. For the first time, the shape of the boat can be seen.

Upright braces are placed against the ribbands to exert a pressure counter to that of the molds. Ralph explains that without upright braces, once the ribs are put in place, you would get a "bunch" in your boat. The lines wouldn't be fair; there would be a bulge.

Ralph and Tim are preparing to replace the molds with frames, or ribs, as they are often called. The ribs will be placed athwartships at right angles to the keel. This part of the construction has been compared to the human rib cage in relation to the backbone.

In the shop there is a large wooden steam box that is heated with a simple hot-water boiler. The oak for the ribs is placed within it for about an hour, the time it takes to heat an inch of frame thickness.

The first rib is set in place amidships. Tim wears gloves to protect his hands as he passes the heated frame to Ralph, who bends it to the inside of the ribbands with pressure from his foot. The frame must touch all the ribbands. Tim clamps each frame to the ribbands as it cools in place. Ralph uses white oak here because it is flexible, yet strong, and can easily take the many fastenings that must be put in for the planking.

Once the frames are in place, planking can begin. The long boards used for planking are called strakes. Ralph starts at the bottom with the first plank next to the keel. This is called the garboard strake. The planks are fitted alternately fore and aft, from one side of the boat to the other, so that the hull will not be pulled out of shape. The ribbands are removed as they get in the way of a plank.

After all the planks are on, Ralph removes the molds. The pure, clean shape of the hull of the Stanley 19 is now visible and ready to be smoothed.

But before the hull is smoothed completely, cotton caulking must be placed between the planks to make the seal watertight. Too much caulking causes the planks to come away from the frames, and too little will loosen and fall out when the planks are wet. Ralph knows from years of experience just how much is enough.

Seams are painted and then smoothed. Knots are carved out and plugged with softwood dowels made of pine. Ralph smoothes off the end of the plug with a chisel, planes it flat, and then sands it for a smooth finish. Everything is done to insure fair lines and a smooth, even hull with no bumps.

To mark the waterline, Ralph and Richard set up level straightedges fore and aft and pull a thin, strong cord taut between them.

Points on the waterline are marked. Ralph takes a moment to check how the Stanley 19 will look when afloat.

A batten is nailed to the hull to connect the points and mark the line. Ralph uses a piece of bent iron to scribe the line on the hull.

To attach the rudder to the hull, Ralph fits the rudder foot into a bronze socket. Above, in the cockpit, Richard is fastening the deck around the rudder post. The deck is made of two layers of plywood glued together to make a continuously even surface with no bumps or ridges. Canvas is then cemented over the wood. After it is stretched tightly and tacked down, it is painted with a good coat of waterproof paint.

The coaming is an oak board that rims the edge of the cockpit to keep water from running in. The boards for the coaming must be steamed so that they will bend easily into place. Ralph and an apprentice stand in the boat while Richard passes the steaming boards to them. It is important to work quickly once the wood is removed from the steam box. The front end is placed first. After the coaming is positioned, clamps hold it securely in place while it cools. A mallet is used to level the coaming so that it sits nearly flush with the underpart of the deck.

The last piece to be added is a toe rail. This is a flexible piece of oak that is added for secure footing when the boat heels and is also a finishing edge for the deck canvas. Seams are painted and smoothed again to ensure a fair hull with no bumps.

Richard has built a simple cabin with a single-planked roof and a sliding hatch. The cabin is just big enough for an overnight trip with a friend or two. A couple of sleeping bags and some provisions can easily be stowed below.

To make a strong mast, Ralph looks for a tree that has grown straight and true, a tree that has been shielded from strong wind from one direction, a tree that has grown without strain or internal stress. The wood must be tough, yet bend easily. The mast for Alex's boat comes from a protected grove of spruce trees on Greening Island, where Alex spends his summers.

After the spruce tree is cut, it must be shaped to form the mast. First the bark is removed. Then the log is planed and tapered top and bottom. The thickest part will go through the deck. The mast is twenty-four feet tall and stepped forward of amidships.

Alex's boat will have a gaff-rigged mainsail and a smaller sail in front called a jib. The jib helps with balance and with sailing into the wind.

Ralph has given Mr. Chase, the sailmaker, a sail plan for the Stanley 19. The sail plan gives the dimensions and shape of the sail. Alex's sail is made of dacron and is 175 feet square. This is not considered a large amount of sail for a 19-footer. The area of the mainsail is low, calculated for added safety and an easy response to the slightest breeze.

The sails are faired off of curved lines on the loft floor. The process is similar to that of lofting a boat. After the sail is cut to shape, it is spread out on the loft floor and sewn on a sewing machine by the sailmaker. In the sail loft different kinds of rope and fabric are stored for use when needed.

At the end of May, Ralph receives another letter from Alex.

Dear Ralph,

School will be over at the beginning of June. I can't wait. I plan to arrive in Southwest Harbor around June 21. I hear the boat looks terrific. Painting it will be my job. I hope that we can do most of the finishing in time for a July 1 launching.

I've been having trouble deciding what to call her, and Dad suggested the steed of another Alexander—Alexander the Great. His name was Bucephalus. It means "swift and spirited." I kind of like that. It might be the perfect name. We'll see when I get there.

My best regards to everyone. Congratulations to you and Marion on Edward's graduation from MIT.

See you, not soon enough.

Love,
Alex

The day before the launch, Ralph and Alex are adjusting the sails and applying last-minute touch-ups with the paintbrush.

Ralph is in the bosun's chair putting up the lazy jack—part of the rigging that makes it safer to hoist or lower the sail. Alex attaches the peak halyard.

Alex and his father carry weight for the ballast from a nearby shed. They have calculated the need for 1,500 pounds of lead weight. Each double weight is twenty pounds. After the job is done, they sit in the boat and relax for a few minutes.

The night before the launch Alex has a pizza and ginger ale next to the boat. He takes his stove, frying pan, and other cooking utensils aboard. He stows his camera. It is after dark when Alex revs the engine of the lobster boat *Annie T.* to head for home. It's time to catch some sleep before morning.

The launch is scheduled for 7:15 A.M., when the tide is high. It will be the low range of high tide, called a neap tide, which comes between the full moon and the new moon. Alex brings the *Annie T.* over from Greening Island when the sky is still gray. Everyone continues to work steadily until the final minutes before the launch. Alex and Ralph appear to be very calm, but Ralph is quiet and isn't smiling as much as he usually does. He seems to be listening to the wind. When Alex's friend Agnes arrives, Ralph and Agnes discuss where to hit the boat for the christening. There is a bowstay wire beneath the bowsprit, so they decide that Agnes will aim the champagne bottle just below it. Agnes practices a few times. She's worried that the bottle won't break at the right moment.

A small crowd of well-wishers have been gathering in the yard despite the early hour. Finally, Ralph decides that the right moment has arrived. The tide will not wait.

Agnes stands close to the boat. "I christen thee *Bucephalus.* May all who sail her, and all who sail under her, sail safely and with grace. May she have fair winds and blue skies on all her voyages, and may they be many." Agnes raises the bottle of champagne and brings it down sharply and neatly on the bow. *Bucephalus* is officially launched.

Getting the boat down the ways is another matter. She is held on a wooden brace called a cradle. Ralph and Richard decide to ballast the cradle to keep it from floating when it hits the water. Richard brings the largest rocks he can find and places them on the cradle. Then, while Tim applies directional pressure with a large stick, Ralph holds the line to keep the cradle straight on the tracks. With a creak *Bucephalus* slides slowly down the ways. At a certain point a line from the *Annie T.* is connected to the stern to quicken the pace and guide *Bucephalus* into the water.

Once the boat is in the water, Ralph begins to smile again. "Alex," he calls. "How bad is she leaking?"

After Alex and Ralph make a trial run on *Bucephalus,* Ralph decides there is too much roll and more ballast is needed. The boat isn't down to her waterline yet and is too tender. Tender means that the boat leans or tips too much because of the pressure of the wind on the sail or the weight of the crew when all stand to one side. Ralph adds another two or three hundred pounds of ballast so that the boat will float level fore and aft and stability will be increased. There is still fine tuning to do and minor adjustments to make.

A party to celebrate the launch is scheduled for later in the day on Greening Island. Alex or his dad will come by the town pier with the *Annie T.* to pick up guests who need a ride.

On the island everyone is gathering wood—all the kindling and dried twigs to be found—to cook the lobster and the hot dogs. Alex's dad has filled large pots with seawater and set them up to boil. Ralph has brought clams. Agnes and other members of the family have brought corn bread and salad and baskets of fruit.

Before the meal Alex and Ralph go for a sail. The extra ballast has improved the roll, and *Bucephalus* holds to her course as steadily as if she were on wheels.

Early the next morning Alex climbs aboard *Bucephalus* for a voyage to Frenchboro, a small island called Outer Long Island by the people of Mt. Desert. As the mainsail furls, a large I is visible. It stands for the first Stanley 19.

Close-hauled on a port tack, Alex remembers something he and Ralph had once talked about.

"When I build a boat, I shape the wood and give it form," Ralph had said. "And over the years I help to keep that vessel afloat. It is a long process. For me, it is a way of life. And the building part is only the beginning."

The wind picks up, and *Bucephalus* is moving more swiftly. Handling just right. Heeling just enough. Not too tender. The ballast perfect.

Alex is thinking, Only the beginning. Yes, it is only the beginning.

GLOSSARY

Aft   Toward the back of the boat

Alee   To the leeward side, away from the wind

Amidships   In or near the middle of a boat, fore to aft or from side to side; the midpoint

Athwartships   Across the vessel from side to side

Ballast   Weight, often iron or lead, carried inside or bolted outside the boat for stability

Batten   In boatbuilding, a long, narrow flexible piece of wood used to draw an exact curve

Beam   The width of a boat

Body plan   A cross-sectional drawing of a boat's lines; usually drawn as a composite with a section of bow and a section of stern drawn from the same baseline

Boom   A spar at the lower edge of a sail used to extend it

Bosun's chair   A portable seat for hoisting people up the mast

Bow   The forward part of a boat

Bowsprit   A large spar projecting from the stem of a ship to carry sail forward and to support the masts by stays

Buoy   A floating navigation marker

Caulking   A waterproofing material, frequently cotton, used to fill the open seams in a boat to make them watertight

Centerboard   A movable keel that may be lowered into the water to keep the boat from slipping sideways when sailing

Closed-course race   A race short enough to be sailed in a morning or an afternoon

Close-hauled   Sailing close to the wind

Coaming   A raised edge around a cockpit or hatch that keeps water out

Cockpit   An open space aft of a decked area from which a small boat is steered

Cradle   A wooden frame supporting a boat when launched

Deck   The permanent roof over a hull

Draft   The depth to which a boat extends below the waterline

Fair   Smooth, without bumps; said of a line or a surface

Frame   The ribs of the boat to which the planking is fastened

Friendship, Maine   A boatbuilding town on the coast of Maine between Pemaquid Point and Rockland

Friendship sloop   A kind of fishing boat built originally in and around Friendship, Maine; wide in the middle with a lot of ballast and a deep keel, particularly safe and adapted to the heavy weather conditions of the Maine coast

Gaff   A spar that extends a fore-and-aft sail of four unequal sides

Garboard   The first plank above the keel

Halyard   A rope to hoist and lower a sail

Heel   A sideways leaning of a boat when under sail

Horn timber   A central part of the keel extending aft from sternpost to transom

Hull   The body of the boat; the basic form

Jib   A triangular sail forward of the foremast

Keel   The backbone of the boat running along the bottom of the hull from stem to stern

Lazy jack   A forked line reaching from the top of the mast to the middle of the boom to hold the sail in place when lowered

Leeward   Away from the wind

Length   The length of the boat not counting the bowsprit

Lines drawing   The entire plan, which includes several views: the elevation, called the profile, shows sheer, keel, stern, and buttocks; the plan shows the sheer in plan and the waterline; the end-on view, or body plan, shows multiple cross sections from a single baseline.

Lofting   The process of drawing the lines of a boat full-scale on the floor

Mainsail   The principal sail on the mainmast

Mast   A vertical spar of metal or wood that supports the boom and the sails

Mold   One of several frames placed on the keel that represent the shape of the boat at specific sections, or stations

Planking   Long strips of wood attached fore and aft to the ribs of the boat; gives the boat strength, makes it watertight, and defines its shape

Port   The left side of a boat when facing the bow

Rabbet   A groove in a plank or timber to accept the edge of a plank; in the keel, receive the molds, or frames

Rib   A transverse member of the frame of a ship that runs from keel to deck and carries the planking

Ribbands   Long strips of flexible wood placed around the molds fore and aft against which the ribs will be set

Rigging   Ropes that secure and/or control masts and sails

Rudder   A vertical piece aft on the hull for steering the boat

Rudder post   A post to which the rudder is connected

Sail   A piece of cloth on the mast to catch the wind

Sail plan   The plan of the dimensions and shape of the sail

Scantlings   The dimensions of parts used in shipbuilding

Schooner   A two-masted sailboat with the tallest mast aft

Sheer   The line where the deck and sides of a boat meet

Sheet   A rope used to control a sail

Single-planked   A single layer of planking

Sloop   A single-masted sailboat with a mainsail and a foresail

Spanish windlass   A winch-like device that holds a vertical and horizontal line taut and allows for further tightening when necessary

Spar   Any wood or metal pole used to hold or give shape to sails

Starboard   The right side of a boat when facing the bow

Stem   The foremost part of the bow

Stern   The rear of the boat

Sternpost   The principal member of the stern extending from keel to deck

Stopwater   A wooden plug used in boatbuilding to keep water from running along the seam between two keel members

Strake   A fore-to-aft plank

Tack   To change direction when sailing upwind by swinging the bow of the boat across the wind

Tender   Little resistance to tipping

Tiller   A handle or lever connected to the rudder to steer the boat

Toe rail   A piece of wood around the edge of the deck that helps to secure footing and is a finishing edge for the deck canvas

Waterline   A painted line marking the level of the water on the hull when the boat is afloat

Ways   Tracks that are used to ease a boat into the water or haul it out; also called skids

Windward   Toward the wind